Selena
the Sleepover Fairy

Daisy Meadows

ORCHARD

www.rainbowmagicbooks.co.uk

Contents

Story One

The Magical Sleeping Bag

The Magical Sleeping Bag

"I can't believe we're going
to a sleepover in the National
Museum!" said Rachel Walker
to her best friend Kirsty Tate as
the coach rumbled down the

motorway. "I can't wait. It's going to be so cool!"

The two best friends were among thirty children taking part in a schools' sleepover and everyone was super excited. After a while, the coach began to slow down.

"We'll stop here for twenty minutes," began Mr Ferguson, one of the teachers in charge. "So keep an eye on your watches." The service station was hidden from the motorway by a line of trees. As Rachel

looked at them, something
sparkled among the leaves.

"That looks like fairy dust!"
she said. The girls were friends
with the fairies, and often
helped out when mischievous
Jack Frost caused them trouble.

As the girls rushed towards the trees, glimmering purple sparkles whizzed around them, and suddenly a fairy appeared, carrying a teddy bear! "Hello," she said in a velvety voice. "I'm Selena the Sleepover Fairy."

She looked worried and the girls gasped as she gave them a warning. "Your sleepover could be at risk because Jack Frost has done something horrible!"

"What do you mean?" Kirsty asked, wide-eyed.

"Last night," explained Selena, "we held a fairy sleepover, but Jack Frost didn't like us having fun so he stole my three precious magical objects, and without them no sleepover will go smoothly."

"What are your magical

objects?" Rachel asked the sad-looking fairy.

"The magical sleeping bag ensures everyone gets a good night's sleep," Selena began. "The  enchanted  games bag makes all games fun and fair, and the sleepover snack box guarantees everyone

 will enjoy
lots of tasty
food."

"We'll
help you find
them," offered Rachel.

"And they may not be
too far away!" added Kirsty,
pointing across to the car
park. They all turned to see
six goblins climbing out of
the coach, carrying rucksacks
and sleeping bags. Jack Frost
had sent his goblin servants to
search for the magical objects!

"Those naughty goblins!" exclaimed Kirsty. As the girls watched, the green mischief-makers scampered into the service station, laden down with luggage.

Kirsty, Rachel and Selena, hidden in Kirsty's hair, hurried

after them. The service station was so busy it was hard to see through the crowds but at last Rachel caught up with them. "That way!" she called. As the girls continued walking, they could hear squabbling goblin voices.

"Get off my sleeping bag!"

"Give it back!"

The goblins pushed each other crossly until one of them staggered into a magazine stand and knocked it over.

The silly goblins quickly

ran off, and this time the girls couldn't keep up with them. They searched everywhere, eventually exploring right at the back of the service station. The lights weren't working and it was very quiet until suddenly they heard a giggle, and tiptoed around a corner. The goblins were all there, settling down inside their stolen sleeping bags. They were having a sleepover of their own!

One silly goblin had a sleeping bag that really didn't

suit him. It was pink, decorated
with hearts and sweets, and was
glowing softly.

"That's my sleeping bag!"
said a delighted Selena.

Rachel and Kirsty gasped

as they stared at the magical sleeping bag. "We can't get it back while there's a goblin inside it!" Rachel whispered.

"I've got an idea," said Kirsty, turning to Selena. "Could you perform a spell to make it really uncomfortable? Then he might get out!"

"Great idea," Selena smiled, waving her wand.

Suddenly the goblin wrinkled his nose. "Yuck! My sleeping bag stinks of strawberries," he complained, quickly clambering out of it.

Rachel and Kirsty ran towards the sleeping bag, but they weren't quick enough. The goblins realised what was happening, all jumped back in together, and zipped it up.

"Give that sleeping bag back!"

exclaimed Rachel. But the silly, rude goblins just stuck out their tongues.

"All right," said Selena, waving her wand over the grinning goblins. "You stay there then."

Gradually, the goblins began to wriggle. "It's very hot in here," said one.

"I can't undo the zip!" complained another. "That tricksy fairy has magicked it shut! We're stuck!"

"Now," began Selena. "Please give back the magical sleeping

bag and everything else you took, and I'll give you your own sleeping bags."

Kirsty bit her lip anxiously.

"I'm too hot!" one goblin exclaimed. "Just let me out! We agree!"

With a wave of her wand, the hot goblins tumbled out of the bag, and with a purple flash, each one had a stinky green sleeping bag under his arm.

"Can you magic them back to the Ice Castle?" Kirsty whispered to Selena.

"I can't," she sighed as they watched the goblins running to the car park and hiding on the coach with the luggage. "But I'll make sure they fall asleep and don't cause any mischief. Thank you for helping me today."

Selena magicked the sleeping bag back to fairy size, then sent all the ordinary sleeping bags and rucksacks safely back to the school coach.

Selena fluttered around in a whirl of violet sparkles. "I'll be back when I've returned the magical sleeping bag to Fairyland," she  smiled at the girls. "After all, we still have to find my other two magical objects!"

"We'll help!" Rachel promised with a big smile.

As the little fairy disappeared, Kirsty looked at her watch.

"Oh, no!" she said, grabbing Rachel's arm. "We've got to get back to the car park!"

They quickly ran towards the coach, climbed on board and dropped into their seats, panting and giggling.

"Just in time, girls!" smiled Mr Ferguson. "Next stop, the National Museum!"

Story Two

The Enchanted
Games Bag

The Enchanted Games Bag

As the coach rolled along,
heading for the museum,
Rachel and Kirsty wondered if
Selena would be there to meet
them. They couldn't wait to see
their fairy friend again.

When they arrived at the museum a little later, everyone eagerly filed off the coach. There were crowds of chattering, excited children everywhere.

"Right, everybody," said Mr Ferguson. "Take your things from the luggage hold and line up in pairs."

"Oh, Kirsty!" Rachel exclaimed. "We have to get to the luggage quickly and check that the goblins aren't up to mischief!"

It seemed to take forever until

the children in front of them
had collected their bags. At last
it was their turn.

"Here are our things,"
whispered Rachel, peering
inside the luggage hold. "But
there are no goblins."

"Selena's spell made the goblins sleep, but they must have got out when the bus stopped!" said Kirsty.

Everyone walked into the museum and, for the moment, the goblins were forgotten.

"Good evening," said a smiling lady. "I'm Charlotte, and you are going to be in the Purple Group."

Rachel and Kirsty listened carefully as Charlotte told them about the treasure hunt.

"Each group must follow

clues to find a letter of the alphabet," she explained. "When the letters are put together, they will spell out a place in the museum. That's where the midnight feast and storytelling will be held!"

Then Charlotte gave them each a purple cap.

"The enchanted games bag is missing," Kirsty whispered to Rachel as they dropped off their bags. "Without it, the treasure hunt will go wrong!"

They followed Charlotte to the Roman Gallery, where she handed an envelope to each pair of children.

"Good luck finding the missing letter!" she smiled.

Kirsty opened the envelope and read out their clue.

Harder than glass and richer than crowns, you'll find me on fingers and fabulous gowns!

"Diamonds are harder than glass," Kirsty whispered.

"Yes!" said Rachel. "But there

are no diamonds in here." She
frowned, looking around. "I
think something's wrong with
the clues."

"Look!" said Kirsty suddenly,
pointing to a Roman vase
nearby. It was glowing! Suddenly
Selena zoomed out of it, and the
girls crouched down, out of sight.

"I've seen the enchanted
games bag!" gushed the tiny
fairy. "A boy wearing a red cap
has it."

"One of the goblins must
have dropped it," said Rachel

thoughfully. "And the boy picked it up."

Suddenly, they spotted someone very short rushing past the door.

"A goblin!" cried Kirsty.

"Let's follow him!" said Rachel.

Selena waved her wand, and the girls were caught in a whirl of tiny stars as they shrank to fairy size.

They zoomed out of the gallery and glimpsed the goblin running down the main staircase. They flew closely behind him and when they reached the bottom, they saw six goblins messing around behind the reception desk! Selena and the girls hid behind a dinosaur model and watched as the goblin they had been following rushed up to the desk.

"I can't find the pesky human child who picked up the fairy bag," he said.

"We'll all come and look," sighed another.

"We must find that boy before the goblins do!" said Selena in an urgent whisper.

The three fairies darted down a long corridor, peering closely at everyone. But nobody was carrying anything that looked magical. Then Rachel noticed a boy standing beside a large dinosaur model. He was carrying a bag, and as she watched, she noticed that it was glowing strongly.

"Look!" Selena said. "The enchanted games bag must be inside!"

But before they could decide

what to do, a goblin leaned
down from the dinosaur and
dipped his hand into the

unzipped bag.

Luckily, just then the boy
strode out of the gallery, with
goblins scurrying after him and

the fairies fluttering above.

Next, the boy paused beside a model of a polar bear, and the girls watched as two goblins scrambled up its back.

Realising what they were going to do, Selena swept her wand over Rachel and Kirsty's heads to make them human-sized again.

"Girls," she whispered to Rachel and Kirsty, who saw what was happening just in time and shouted to the boy, "Look out!"

The boy whipped around and the goblin landed on the ground with a furious squawk.

"Give me that bag NOW!" he demanded rudely. The boy looked angry.

"I found it, so it's finders keepers!" he retorted.

"Excuse me," said Rachel.

"Oh, hello," the boy said, turning round to face Rachel and Kirsty. "Thank you for warning me."

"You're welcome," she replied. "You see, we've been looking for you too. I think you've got our friend's bag, and she really needs it back."

The boy stared at them thoughtfully, and then looked at the green-hatted goblin sulking nearby. "This boy's been trying to take it from me too. It must be very special."

"It is," said Kirsty gently.

The boy reached into his travel bag, and drew out the games bag. Smiling broadly, he held it out to Rachel. The goblin snorted with rage.

As the boy said goodbye and headed back to find his group, Selena hovered in front of the girls. With a flick of her wand, the enchanted games bag returned to fairy size, and she smiled at Rachel and Kirsty.

"Thank you for persuading him to give back the magic bag," she said.

"You're welcome," replied Rachel. "Are you taking it back to Fairyland?"

"Yes," Selena said. "But I'll be back. We still have the

sleepover snack box to find!"

As the little fairy

disappeared in a flurry of
pinky-purple dust, Rachel and
Kirsty wandered back to the
Roman Gallery.

When they arrived, Mr
Ferguson was looking very

pleased.

"Charlotte has found some brand-new sets of clues," he told them. Now that everything was back to normal, the groups set off on their treasure hunts again. Altogether they found five letters.

Everyone gathered in the entrance hall and studied the letters together. "Who will be first to put the letters in the right order?" Charlotte asked.

"It spells 'crypt'," called out the boy who had found the

enchanted games bag.

"Correct," said Charlotte, sounding impressed.

Rachel and Kirsty looked at each other. A midnight feast in a crypt? How exciting!

Story Three

The Sleepover Snack Box

The Sleepover Snack Box

Charlotte handed each of the
children a glass lantern. "It's dark
in the crypt," she smiled. There
were lots of gasps and giggles
and they followed Charlotte
down a winding staircase.

It grew colder and darker
as they travelled deeper
underground. At last they
reached an old, wooden door.
Charlotte pushed it open, it gave
a loud *CREEEAAAKK!* and
they faced a long passageway.

"This is where we keep all the exhibits that aren't being used," Charlotte said. In the dim light from their lanterns, the girls saw mysterious boxes and tall vases. There were lots of strange shapes covered in white sheets. The long snake of children wound through more dusty passages until they found themselves in a big room.

A man was sitting, smiling, on an ornate chair.

"This is Zack the Storyteller," Charlotte explained to everyone. As the children moved towards him, Charlotte peered behind a curtain and Rachel and Kirsty caught a glimpse of a long, empty wooden table. Charlotte looked worried as she hurried over to Zack. "There's a bit of a problem," they heard her say. "The feast isn't ready. Could you start the story while I go and sort it out?"

"This must be because the sleepover snack box is still missing!" whispered Rachel.

"Welcome to the crypt," said Zack in a rich, warm voice.

Rachel started listening to the story, but Kirsty was distracted. She kept thinking that someone was behind her. Eventually she turned her head, and saw a spiky-headed shadow!

She quickly nudged Rachel but the strange shadow had completely disappeared.

"Maybe it was the lantern light making funny shapes on the wall?" Rachel suggested. Looking at her own lantern, she gasped. It was shining very brightly, and suddenly Selena the Sleepover Fairy shot out!

"I have news!" she said. "Jack Frost is so fed up with the silly goblins losing everything, he's taken the sleepover snack box himself!"

"I think he's here!" whispered Kirsty. "I just saw his shadow."

"He's searching for the goblins!" Selena realised.

"We have to find him!" whispered Rachel urgently.

"And the sleepover snack box!" added Kirsty.

The girls looked around. Zack was well into his story now, and everyone's attention was on him. They crept after Selena into a far corner, and the fairy waved her tiny wand. There was a faint musical sound, and the girls shrank to fairy size, along with their

lanterns. "We must look
like tiny fireflies!"
giggled
Rachel as
they rose
up into
the air.

Flying
close
together,
the three
friends made
their way down
a long, dark passage.

Suddenly, they heard a crash

and a loud squawk.

"It sounded like a goblin!" cried Selena.

As the fairies eyes got used to the dim light, they saw that a jumble of packing boxes had toppled onto two goblins. One was rubbing a large red bump on his head. The other was rubbing his foot.

"Shhh!" said a third. "Do you want Jack Frost to hear us?"

"You said there was going to be a wonderful midnight feast, but it's cold and dark, and I'm

hungry!" grumbled the first
goblin angrily.

"Come on," whispered
Selena. "Jack Frost's not here.
Let's look somewhere else."

They flew back along the tunnel and out into the main room. Suddenly, Rachel gave a cry. "Look!" she whispered, pointing.

Jack Frost was skulking in the shadows, carrying the sleepover snack box under his arm!

"We have to get him away from the other children," said Kirsty. "They would be really scared if they spotted him!"

"Why is he just standing there?" asked Selena.

"I think he wants to hear Zack's story!" said Rachel.

"I've got an idea," said Kirsty to Selena. "Could you use your magic to make our voices sound like goblins? Then Jack Frost might follow us."

Selena waved her wand, and the girls swooped down.

"Silly old Jack Frost!" said Rachel, giggling like a goblin.

Jack Frost's head whipped around, but of course, he couldn't see any goblins.

The girls zoomed into the tunnel entrance.

"Over here!" teased Kirsty, waving her arms in the air, just as Zack reached a very spooky part of his story.

The light from Rachel's lantern cast Kirsty's shadow onto the wall, making it look huge and monstrous. Jack Frost gave a cry, dropped the box and ran away! His terrified scream was so loud, the goblins heard it and thought it was a ghost. They scampered out of the tunnel after him.

"Thank goodness!" said Rachel with a smile. "Jack Frost and the goblins have gone, and we've found the sleepover snack box."

"You've both been wonderful, girls!" said Selena, hugging them tightly. "I am so happy to have all my magical objects back where they belong!"

Selena transformed the sleepover snack box to its Fairyland size with a touch of her sparkly wand. Kirsty and Rachel gave her a big smile.

Then the fairy made the two
girls human size again.

"It's nice to have my own
voice back!" laughed Kirsty.

"Goodbye, and thank you,"
said Selena with a beaming
smile. The air filled with a
shimmering golden fairy dust,

and Selena was gone.

The girls slipped back into the hall just as the story ended and Charlotte appeared with trays of delicious-smelling food. There were bowls of yummy strawberries and masses of iced cupcakes.

After the feast, Charlotte announced it was time for bed. But there were groans from everyone.

"...after a game of hide-and-seek, of course!" Charlotte said with a laugh.

"I'm glad we found all
the magical objects in time,"
Rachel said. "Now we can
enjoy the rest of the sleepover!
It's the perfect end to a truly
magical adventure!"

**If you enjoyed this story,
you may want to read**

Mia the Bridesmaid Fairy
Early Reader

Here's how the story begins...

"I can't wait for next
Saturday!" said Rachel Walker
excitedly to her best friend,
Kirsty Tate. Esther, Kirsty's
cousin, was getting married,
and they were both going to
be bridesmaids!

The girls were staying in
the pretty village of Kenbury,

where the wedding was to take place. As they stood looking at the church, they saw people arriving in their best clothes.

"There must be another wedding today!" cried Kirsty.

Suddenly, a cream car drew up, and a smart chauffeur jumped out and opened the back door. Inside, the girls could see a woman wearing a frothy white dress.

"It's the bride!" Rachel exclaimed. "Isn't she lovely?"

When all the guests had

gone into the church, the girls carefully walked across the road to meet Kirsty's aunt at the wedding shop.

"Girls, come and try on your dresses," said Aunt Isabel as soon as they opened the door. Bella, who ran the shop, was holding up two exquisite dresses. The girls gasped in delight.

"Oh, they're beautiful!" Rachel whispered, as they got changed and stood in front of the mirror.

"You both look lovely!" cried Aunt Isabel.

Bella checked the dresses fitted, before the girls got dressed again and began exploring. At the front of the shop was a table filled with wedding accessories, so they dashed over to have a look.

Read
Mia the Bridesmaid Fairy
Early Reader
to find out
what happens next!

Learn to read with

RAINBOW magic™

- Rainbow Magic Early Readers are easy-to-read versions of the original books

- Perfect for parents to read aloud and for newly confident readers to read along

- Remember to enjoy reading together. It's never too early to share a story!

Everybody loves Daisy Meadows!

'I love your books' – Jasmine, Essex

'You are my favourite author' – Aimee, Surrey

'I am a big fan of Rainbow Magic!' – Emma, Hertfordshire

Meet the first
Rainbow Magic fairies

Can you find one with your name?
There's a fairy book for everyone at
www.rainbowmagicbooks.co.uk

Let the magic begin!

RAINBOW magic

Become a

Rainbow Magic

fairy friend and be the first to
see sneak peeks of new books.

There are lots of special offers and exclusive
competitions to win sparkly
Rainbow Magic prizes.

Sign up today at
www.rainbowmagicbooks.co.uk